Es primavera, querido dragón

It's Spring,
Dear Dragon

por/by Margaret Hillert
ilustrado por/Illustrated by David Schimmell

NORWOOD HOUSE PRESS

La serie para lectores principiantes es una colección de lecturas cuidadosamente escritas, muchas de las cuales ustedes recordarán de su propia infancia. Cada libro comprende palabras de uso frecuente en español e inglés y, a través de la repetición, le ofrece al niño la oportunidad de practicarlas. Los detalles adicionales de las ilustraciones refuerzan la historia y le brindan la oportunidad de ayudar a su niño a desarrollar el lenguaje oral y la comprensión.

Primero, léale el cuento al niño; después deje que él lea las palabras con las que está familiarizado y pronto, podrá leer solito todo el cuento. En cada paso, elogie el esfuerzo del niño para que se sienta más confiado como lector independiente. Hable sobre las ilustraciones y anime al niño a relacionar el cuento con su propia vida.

Sobre todo, la parte más importante de la experiencia de la lectura es ¡divertirse y disfrutarla!

Shannon Cannon

Shannon Cannon
Consultora de lectoescritura

The *Beginning-to-Read* series is a carefully written collection of readers, many of which you may remember from your own childhood. This book, *Dear Dragon's Day with Father*, was written over 30 years after the first *Dear Dragon* books were published. The *New Dear Dragon* series features the same elements of the earlier books, such as text comprised of common sight words. These sight words provide your child with ample practice reading the words that appear most frequently in written text. The many additional details in the pictures enhance the story and offer the opportunity for you to help your child expand oral language skills and develop comprehension.

Begin by reading the story to your child, followed by letting him or her read familiar words and soon your child will be able to read the story independently. At each step of the way, be sure to praise your reader's efforts to build his or her confidence as an independent reader. Discuss the pictures and encourage your child to make connections between the story and his or her own life.

Above all, the most important part of the reading experience is to have fun and enjoy it!

Shannon Cannon,
Literacy Consultant

Norwood House Press • P.O. Box 316598 • Chicago, Illinois 60631
For more information about Norwood House Press please visit our website at *www.norwoodhousepress.com* or call 866-565-2900.

LIBRARY OF CONGRESS CATALOGING-IN-PUBLICATION DATA
Hillert, Margaret.
  [It's spring, dear dragon. Spanish & English]
  Es primavera, querido dragón = It's spring, dear dragon / por/by Margaret Hillert ; ilustrado por/illustrated David Schimmell ; [translated by Eida del Risco].
    p. cm. -- (A beginning-to-read book)
  Includes word list.
  Summary: "A boy and his pet dragon enjoy a spring day by playing outside and exploring all the season has to offer Carefully translated to include English and Spanish text "--Provided by publisher.
  ISBN-13: 978-1-59953-471-8 (library edition : alk. paper)
  ISBN-10: 1-59953-471-1 (library edition : alk. paper)
  [1. Dragons--Fiction. 2. Spring--Fiction. 3. Spanish language materials--Bilingual.]
  I. Schimmell, David, ill. II. Del Risco, Eida. III. Title. IV. Title: It's spring, dear dragon. V. Title: It is spring, dear dragon.
  PZ73.H557204 2011
  [E]--dc23
                                        2011016648

Manufactured in the United States of America in North Mankato, Minnesota.
178N—072011

¡Ay, no!
Mira la lluvia.
Esto no es bueno.
No podemos salir.

Oh, no!
Look at the rain.
This is not good.
We cannot go out.

No puedes salir
pero esto es bueno.
Mira afuera.

You cannot go out
but this is good.
Look out here.

¡Ay, sí!
Veo algo.
Algo pequeño y verde.

Oh, yes!
I see something.
Something little and green.

5

Las cositas verdes
se pondrán grandes
    y bonitas.
Ya verás.

The little green things
will get big and pretty.
You will see.

Marzo
March

D	L	M	M	J	V	S
S	M	T	W	T	F	S
		1	2	3	4	5
6	7	8	9	10	11	12
13	14	15	16	17	18	19
20	21	22	23	24	25	26
27	28	29	30	31		

¿Así, mamá?
¿Así?

Like this, Mother?
Like this?

Sí, eso está bien.

Ahora mira lo que tengo para ti.

Graciosos sombreros verdes y galletas verdes.

Yes, that is good.

Now see what I have for you—

funny green hats and green cookies.

¡Caramba! Qué bueno está esto.
Eres una buena mamá.

Oh, boy. This is so good.
You are a good mother.

Eh, mira.
Mira afuera ahora.
Mira bien, bien alto.
Qué bonito es
el arco iris.

Oh, oh.
Look out there now.
Look way, way up.
How pretty the
rainbow is.

Ahora podemos salir.
Será bueno ver a los amigos.

Now we can go out.
It will be good to see friends.

14

Haz esto.
Haz esto.
Salta, salta, salta.
¡Qué divertido!

Do this.
Do this.
Jump, jump, jump.
What fun!

¿Qué es eso?
¿Cómo se juega a eso?
Parece divertido.

What is this?
How do you play this?
It looks like fun.

Ah, ya veo.
Yo puedo hacer salir a la roja.

Oh, I see.
I can make the red one go out.

Las niñas juegan bien a eso.
Yo quiero hacerlo.

The girls are good at that.
I want to do it.

Ay, ay.
Creo que no lo hago muy bien.

Oh, oh.
I guess I am not so good at this.

Mira eso.

Es bueno ver eso.

Me pone contento.

Look at that.

It is good to see that.

It makes me happy.

Mira lo que come.
¡Es bueno para él,
pero no para mí!

See what it eats.
It is good for him
but not for me!

Y mira aquí.
Qué conejito tan bonito.
¡Puede correr y saltar!

And look here.
What a pretty bunny.
It can run and jump!

¿Vendrá a mi casa?
¿Tendrá algo para mí?

Will it come to my house?
Will it have something for me?

Ay, ay.
Tenemos que irnos.
Corre, corre, corre.

Oh, oh.
We have to go.
Run, run, run.

Tú estás conmigo
y yo estoy contigo.
Qué buen amigo eres, querido dragón.

Here you are with me.
And here I am with you.
What a good friend you are, dear dragon.

The following activities support the findings of the National Reading Panel that determined the most effective components for reading instruction are: Phonemic Awareness, Phonics, Vocabulary, Fluency, and Text Comprehension.

Phonemic Awareness: The /spr/ and /str/ consonant blends

1. Say the word spring and ask your child to repeat the /**spr**/ sound.

2. Say the word string and ask your child to repeat the /**str**/ sound.

3. Explain to your child that you are going to say some words and you would like her/him to show you one finger if the sound in the word is /**spr**/ as in spring or two fingers if the sound in the word is /**str**/, as in string.

spray	strap	spree	sprint	stream
straw	spruce	strange	stripe	sprinkle

Phonics: Consonant clusters spr- and str-

1. Demonstrate how to form the letters **spr** and **str** for your child.

2. Have your child practice writing **spr** and **str** at least three times each.

3. Divide a piece of paper in half by folding it the long way. Draw a line on the fold. Turn it so that the paper has two columns. Write the words spring and string at the top of the columns.

4. Write the words above on separate index cards. Ask your child to sort the words based on the **spr** and **str** spellings.

Word Work: ABC Order

1. Ask your child to recite the alphabet. Write the letters of the alphabet on a piece of paper and sing the alphabet song together while pointing at the letters.

2. Write the following words on separate index cards: am, and, are, be, big, boy, can, cookies, cupcake, for, friend, funny, girls, green, guess,

happy, hat, have, like, little, look, man, me, mother, pit, play, pretty, see, some, spring, that, there, thing, we, what, will.

3. Place the words am, big, can, hat, look, man, play, see, that, will (mix up the order) in front of your child. Ask your child to name the first letter in each word.

4. Tell your child that you are going to work together to put the words in alphabetical order by looking at the first letter in each word. Help your child put the words in order.

5. Next, put the words for, friend, funny (mix up the order) in front of your child.

6. Tell your child that when words begin with the same letter, we put them in order based on the second letter. Help your child put the words in alphabetical order.

7. Sort the cards based on the first letter. Shuffle them and put them in piles, faced down. Have your child practice putting the words from each group in alphabetical order.

8. Challenge: Shuffle all the cards together and ask your child to put all of the words in alphabetical order.

Fluency: Shared Reading

1. Reread the story to your child at least two more times while your child tracks the print by running a finger under the words as they are read. Ask your child to read the words he or she knows with you.

2. Reread the story taking turns, alternating readers between sentences or pages of the story.

Text Comprehension: Discussion Time

1. Ask your child to retell the sequence of events in the story.

2. To check comprehension, ask your child the following questions:

   • Why couldn't the boy go outside at the beginning of the story?

   • What holiday were they celebrating with the green hats and cookies?

   • What appeared after it stopped raining?

Margaret Hillert ha escrito más de 80 libros para niños que están aprendiendo a leer. Sus libros han sido traducidos a muchos idiomas y han sido leídos por más de un millón de niños de todo el mundo. De niña, Margaret empezó escribiendo poesía y más adelante siguió escribiendo para niños y adultos. Durante 34 años, fue maestra de primer grado. Ya se retiró, y ahora vive en Michigan donde le gusta escribir, dar paseos matinales y cuidar a sus tres gatos.

Photograph by Glenna Washburn

ABOUT THE AUTHOR Margaret Hillert has written over 80 books for children who are just learning to read. Her books have been translated into many different languages and over a million children throughout the world have read her books. She first started writing poetry as a child and has continued to write for children and adults throughout her life. A first grade teacher for 34 years, Margaret is now retired from teaching and lives in Michigan where she likes to write, take walks in the morning, and care for her three cats.

ACERCA DEL ILUSTRADOR David Schimmell fue bombero durante 23 años, al cabo de los cuales guardó las botas y el casco y se dedicó a trabajar como ilustrador. David ha creado las ilustraciones para la nueva serie de Querido dragón, así como para muchos otros libros. David nació y se crió en Evansville, Indiana, donde aún vive con su esposa, dos hijos, un nieto y dos nietas.

ABOUT THE ILLUSTRATOR David Schimmell served as a professional firefighter for 23 years before hanging up his boots and helmet to devote himself to work as an illustrator. David has happily created the illustrations for the New Dear Dragon books as well as many other books throughout his career. Born and raised in Evansville, Indiana, he lives there today with his wife, two sons, a grandson and two granddaughters.